For Ginger, and Emily
—A.D.
To Winnie, with love
—H.C.

City Chicken • Text copyright © 2003 by Arthur Dorros • Illustrations
copyright © 2003 by Henry Cole • Printed in the U.S.A. • All rights
reserved. • www.harperchildrens.com • Library of Congress Cataloging-
in-Publication Data • Dorros, Arthur. • City chicken / by Arthur Dorros;
illustrated by Henry Cole. • p. cm. • Summary: Egged on by the cat
next door, a chicken from the city visits the country to see what
she's been missing, and finds that it's not "all it's cracked up to be." •
ISBN 0-06-028482-X — ISBN 0-06-028483-8 (lib. bdg.) [1. Chickens—
Fiction. 2. City and town life—Fiction. 3. Country life—Fiction.
4. Animals—Fiction. 5. Humorous stories.] I. Cole, Henry, 1955– ill.
II. Title. • PZ7.D7294 Ci 2003 00-066363 • [E]—dc21 •
Typography by Elynn Cohen 1 2 3 4 5 6 7 8 9 10 ❖ First Edition

City Chicken

by Arthur Dorros
illustrated by Henry Cole

HarperCollinsPublishers

Henry was a chicken. Her name was short for Henrietta. She lived in the city in a chicken coop behind Alex's house.

Alex visited Henry every day. He took care of
her and collected her eggs. All the eggs were blue.
"Amazing," said Alex.

"Weird," said Lucy,
the cat from next door.

"What's a chicken like you doing laying eggs around here?"

"I live here. Chickens lay eggs. Mine are blue."

"Don't get ruffled," said Lucy.

"That's what chickens do," clucked Henry, ruffling her feathers.

"All right," said Lucy. "But chickens usually live in the country, where it is peaceful, with cows and—"

"What's a cow?" asked Henry.

"Cows live in the country. They eat grass, and milk comes out. You'd have to see it to believe it."

Henry ate all the food that Alex brought—pizza, strawberries, watermelon, and waffles.

"You eat like a horse," Lucy said to Henry.

"I eat like a chicken," clucked Henry. "What's a horse?"

"Horses live in the country. They are huge and brown and let people jump on their backs. You'd have to see it to believe it."

Henry scratched in the garden, looking for worms. Dirt and stones and grass flew everywhere.

"You're as dirty as a pig," said Lucy.

"What is a pig?" asked Henry.

"Pigs live in the country. They are pink and stick their noses in the dirt. You wouldn't believe what pigs are like."

"Enough!" clacked Henry. "I am going to the country to see everything for myself!" She leaped to the roof and flew the coop.

Henry was not the best flier. She flapped a short way, then had to rest. She dropped in on a statue covered with pigeons and white speckles.

"You are a strange-looking bird," said a pigeon.

"I am a chicken," said Henry.

"Whatever you say, honey," cooed the pigeon.

"I am trying to get to the country."

"The way you fly, maybe you should take the bus," said the pigeon. "A bus stops over there."

"Thank you," said Henry.

"Don't mention it," said the pigeon.

"I already did," said Henry.

Henry hopped on the bus.

"Exact change only," the bus driver said.

Henry did not have change. She had feathers.

She put one in the coin slot.

"What a turkey," said a dog.
"Chicken," said Henry.
"I am not," barked the dog.
"I am," cackled Henry.
"Stop!" called the dog.

The bus driver pulled over. So did the bus.
"Hey chicken, you'll have to cross the road to get to the country," said the dog.
Henry strutted off.

Henry perched on a little hill to look around.

"Watch where you're going!" piped an ant.

"I am going to the country," clucked Henry.

"My aunt and uncle live in the country," said the ant. "Lots of ants live in the country. Lots of chickens, too."

"Where is the country these days?" Henry asked.

"It's where the city isn't," the ant replied. "Here's a truck that goes to the country. And they serve great meals on board!"

The food was all mixed together and smelled bad.

"We're here," said the ant as the truck bumped to a stop.

"The country looks bigger than I thought," Henry said. She hopped off the truck and started across a field.

"*Neigh*," said a large animal chewing grass.

Henry remembered that cows eat grass. "What a funny-looking cow," clucked Henry.

Henry saw huge animals in a pen. She
remembered that horses are huge and brown.
"Why are those horses rolling in the mud?" asked
Henry. "Dust makes a better bath." She bathed
herself with dust and waddled off.

It started to rain.
Henry heard *perawk, puk, puk, perawk* from
inside a big building.
She looked for a way to go in.

It was not like the coop Alex had built, with a door just for Henry.

Two creaky doors swung open, and a machine roared out.

There were bright lights inside, and hundreds and hundreds of chickens.

Each chicken had its own small space.
"It looks like a city of chickens," thought Henry.

Henry saw an
empty space and
jumped into it.
"Hello, I'm Henry.
Who are you?"
"Duck!" cackled the
chicken.
"You look like a chicken to
me," said Henry.
Motors whirred, gears rattled,
chains clanked.
"Duck, or you'll get pelted with
flying corn!" Corn showered down from
machines above.

Henry wondered who was throwing corn at her.

"Hello," Henry clucked to the other chickens.

"*Perawk*, we're too busy to talk," squawked the chickens. They were busy laying eggs.

White eggs and brown eggs rolled down a track. One blue egg rolled down, too. Henry had laid it.

A conveyor belt carried the eggs away. Henry fell onto it. She was flipped around and up and down.

Lights flashed. "This is not the place for me!" Henry decided.

WHAP! The lid of an egg box almost trapped her.
She heard a man's voice. "This one's ready for the city."
"You'd better believe it," thought Henry.

She hopped into the truck and hid among the boxes.

It was a long ride to the city. When the truck stopped, Henry scrambled out. She stretched her wings and flapped home.

"She's back!" exclaimed Alex.

"Here come the eggs," said Lucy.

"First comes the chicken, then the eggs," said Henry.

"Was the country all it was cracked up to be?" asked Lucy.

"It was different," said Henry. "But it was not the place for me."

"I know another place," said Lucy. "The first chicken is about to be blasted into space with the astronauts."

"What's an astronaut?" asked Henry.

"Someone who is rocketed into space. Astronauts wear bubbles on their heads and explore strange planets. You wouldn't believe it . . ."

"Sounds out of this world," said Henry.